One of the animals visiting Bambi was a funny gray bunny.

"Hiya, Bambi," said the little rabbit, who was standing beside his mother and sisters. "I'm thumpin' all the time, so everybody calls me Thumper! Come on, Bambi. I'll show you around!"

And so Thumper became Bambi's very first friend.

Bambi and Thumper went exploring. "The forest is a wonderful place!" thought Bambi, looking at the upside-down opossums.

Thumper taught Bambi the names of things in the forest. "Those are birds," Thumper said.

"*Bir-duh*," said Bambi slowly.

The young prince had spoken his first word!

"And these are flowers," Thumper whispered. "They're pretty."

Bambi sniffed. Then his nose touched something warm and fuzzy.

"*Flower!*" said Bambi, as a little black-and-white head popped up from the petals.

"That's not a flower," said Thumper, laughing so hard he could barely speak. "That's a skunk!"

"I don't care," said the shy little skunk, with his eyes twinkling. "He can call me a flower if he wants to."

"Flower," Bambi repeated.

So Flower the skunk got his name.

Bambi was exploring a meadow pond when, suddenly, a big, green bullfrog hopped into the water.

Bambi leaned over for a closer look. When the ripples cleared, he saw something staring at him. He jumped back. It was another fawn!

"Don't be afraid, Bambi," his mother said. "You are just seeing yourself in the water."

While Thumper and his sisters chased each other in the grass, Bambi met another deer—a female fawn.

"This is Faline," said Bambi's mother. "She wants to be your friend."

"Hello," whispered Bambi in a small, small voice.

"Come and play, Bambi!" said Faline.

Bambi followed her, flying over the meadow. And they became good friends.

Bambi's first spring was such a wonderful time! Flowers were blooming, leaves sprouted on the trees, and birds sang "tweet-tweet, tweet-tweet."

Bambi romped through the forest with Thumper, Faline, and Flower. He knew that they would all be friends forever.